The Shadow Man

Carole Lloyd

Illustrated by
Anthony Kerins

RED FOX

For Peter

A Red Fox Book

Published by Random House Children's Books
20 Vauxhall Bridge Road, London SW1V 2SA

A division of Random House UK Ltd
London Melbourne Sydney Auckland
Johannesburg and agencies throughout the world

First published in 1991 by Julia MacRae Books

Red Fox edition 1994

7 9 10 8 6

Printed and bound in Great Britain
by Cox & Wyman Ltd, Reading, Berkshire

RANDOM HOUSE UK Limited Reg. No. 954009

ISBN 0 09 997200 X

Contents

Chapter 1   5

Chapter 2   17

Chapter 3   24

Chapter 4   35

Chapter 5   41

Chapter 6   54

Also by Carole Lloyd

The Charlie Barber Treatment
Speccy Four-Eyes

Chapter 1

The walk home from school was always the same at the end of the week and he felt that he wanted to get away from the jabbering of the other boys with their one-track minds.

"What d'you reckon for tomorrow?"

"Four-nil at least, my brother says. United can't lose."

"Can't lose!" they all agreed.

"Going to the match then, Tommo?"

He was tempted to ask which match but thought better of it. There was only one team that mattered around here. He'd supported them too, last season and the one before, but now he didn't much care whether they topped the League or got beamed up by the Starship Enterprise. He'd grown out of it. What was so clever about kicking a ball around a field? Grown men playing kids' games, that's what it was!

"No. I'll probably be busy tomorrow," he said.

"Go on," Wes said. "It'll be great. They'll win dead easy, I reckon." Matt shrugged. "You can come with my dad and me if you like," Wes offered.

"No," Matt repeated, "but thanks anyway." Just before he turned off into the road where he lived Wes gave him a playful push.

"You're weird, you are, Tommo. See ya Monday."

He was glad to be nearly home. At the end of each day Matt liked to give himself a little oasis of peace. He rarely dared to stretch it to more than fifteen or twenty minutes but they were minutes when everything was his. He could raid the biscuit tin, sprawl on the sofa without taking his shoes off or practise imaginary conversations, trying out all the things that he would never dare to say to people's faces.

But tonight Sara was already waiting. She came

careering down the street towards him, her hair like a pale golden pennant streaming behind her.

"Matty, Matty," she called. "Ian's here and he's going to take me swimming." Swimming, by which she meant bobbing about with her armbands on, was her latest craze. She caught at his sleeve, gripping the fabric of his blazer like she used to do when she was really little and had been afraid of losing him in a crowd, but Matt pulled free. He didn't want her hanging on, dragging at his arm. He didn't want their private business announced in the street and, more than that, he didn't want his pet-name broadcast to the world. Outside he was Matt or Thompson or Tommo, never Matty. He hoped no-one had heard.

"Why aren't you at Mrs Anwar's?" he said. "You're supposed to stay there till I come for you." When Sara didn't answer he glanced sideways but he couldn't see her expression, only the tips of her ears poking through the thin curtains of hair, and he was suddenly sorry for being mean.

"How's the wound?" he enquired.

"Better," she said. "Look," and she turned towards him, pushing up her sleeve to show him the long, angry graze.

"You're on the mend," he said, "but try walking instead of running everywhere in future."

"It stopped hurting ages ago," she explained, "when Ian put some ornament on."

"Ointment," he said.

"Ian said ornament."

Matt frowned but didn't argue. Ian probably had. He was always playing around with words to make her giggle and the pair of them now inhabited a world where you watched the veletision or had florncakes for breakfast. It had all begun when Sara found a caterpillar. Far better, Ian had suggested, that caterpillars should grow into flutterbies, in view of the way they spent their brief existence. He

had even convinced Sara that ladies carried 'hambags' because in olden days they had used them to bring home the bacon.

It was all very silly and Matt did not approve. Sara was too young to be confused with lies. She couldn't even spell the proper words.

"What's he doing here at this time, anyway?"

"Dunno," she said.

"Is Mum home?"

"No. It's not time."

"So who let him in then?" He could see the front door left wide open for anyone to stare through.

"You?" She nodded uncertainly. "You must always wait next door until I get home," Matt insisted and she didn't understand why he sounded so cross with her.

"Don't have to!"

"Yes you do! How many times do you have to be told? You're to stay with Mrs Anwar till I get back. That's the rule." Matt felt his irritation churn into a great surge of anger. How could he be responsible for her if she wouldn't even do as she was told?

"What have you done with the key?" he said and as she raced ahead of him towards the house, he knew that she hadn't put it back in its hiding place.

He was just about to follow her in when she slammed the door. He swore under his breath and hammered on the glass with his knuckles.

"Come on," he shouted. "Open it." He could see her skipping around in the hallway and he wanted to scream at her, but there were people in the street and he felt foolish, trapped outside in public view. He couldn't even yell through the letter-box without getting down on his knees on the pavement. Instead he kicked the flap furiously while Sara, safe on the other side, pressed her face to one of the whorled panes. It made her look grotesque, like a goblin behind the thick glass, until he brought his palm down suddenly across it and she backed away. He had just raised his fist again to beat at the wooden frame when a dark shape gathered and grew to fill the space. The door swung open and Ian beamed down at him. Some day Matt intended to ask him if his teeth were false but this wasn't the moment. Instead Matt pretended to be surprised to see their visitor.

"Hello," he said. "Wasn't expecting you till Sunday."

"Just dropped in," Ian explained.

"Mum won't be home for ages yet."

"I know," he replied. "That's OK."

Ian sauntered back down the hall and into the living room, giving Matt a chance to enter his own house and shut the front door. He dumped his bag on the stairs. He would make Sara move it later. Tidying up was her job.

He followed them into the living room and its smallness still shocked him, especially after a day in lofty classrooms. Though at first it had seemed cosy and safe, like a burrow that they could hide in, he was beginning to resent the confines of the little house. Sometimes he felt he couldn't breathe when everyone was in it. To let in the light they had replaced the front door with a new one, like a bow window with squares of heavy gnarled glass,

but he was beginning to resent that too. He hated the way Sara's friends would cup their hands around their eyes to peer in, and it was through this glass that Ian had unexpectedly loomed one evening, a gigantic silhouette between the street lamp and the house. Matt had been half-afraid to open the door.

"Good evening. You must be Matthew. I'm Ian. Is your mother ready or shall I come in and wait?"

"She's n. . . nearly ready," he'd stuttered but let him in anyway, breaking the rules. When his mother had said she was going out with a friend he had assumed that she meant with a woman. It had happened months ago but Matt could still picture it.

Ian had come straight in and sprawled across the little two-seater settee, just as if he owned the place, and by the time Mum appeared, ready to go, he was half-way through *Little Red Riding Hood* with Sara curled happily on his knee. Matt had been left to finish the story, put his sister to bed and to reassure her that neither grandmothers nor little girls could get eaten by a wolf with grinning teeth and a good line in chat.

Now Ian was lounging in his usual place and Sara rushed to sit beside him, out of Matt's reach.

"Well, Matt, had a good day?" Ian asked.

"S'pose so."

"And what about you, young lady? How was your day?" Ian gave her knee a quick squeeze.

"We had races," she said, "and I came first."

"Good girl," he replied. "Do people who come first deserve a prize?" She nodded. "Go and open those chocolates then and you can pass them round."

Matt had already noticed the large box of chocolates, the bottle of wine wrapped in pink tissue paper and a tiny parcel on the sideboard, but he'd decided to ignore them.

"What time did you get here?" he asked.

"About half an hour ago. Bit longer maybe."

"He picked me up from school," said Sara, "and we went to the swings."

Matt sighed. "You're supposed to come straight home, without fail."

"I do," she said.

"You're not allowed to come through the park," he explained. "You know that."

"I'm sure she wouldn't on her own, would you, poppet?" Ian tucked a strand of hair behind her ear and a chocolate into her mouth. Sara immediately helped herself to another one, clutching it in her hand for later, before offering the box to Matt.

"No thanks," he said.

"You're not on a diet, are you?" Ian asked.

"Mummy is," said Sara. "Matty's all skinny already."

"No more before tea," Matt said, trying to take the box from her.

"Ian says I can."

"He said you could have one, not handfuls." She crammed the second one into her mouth quickly before he could take it from her, smearing her face with a chocolatey hand. "Come on. You can help me make some tea and I'll clean you up." Matt wanted to get her out of the room. He couldn't deal with her in front of Ian.

"Don't have to," she retorted.

"Oh, yes you do," Ian said. "You're all sticky," and Sara led the way meekly into the kitchen.

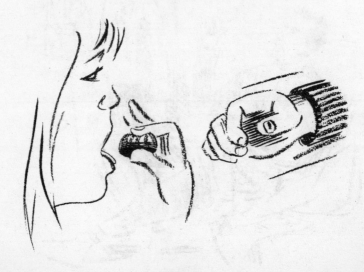

Chapter 2

"How come you do what he says but not what I say?" Matt asked her as she struggled under a damp dishcloth. He held on to her and rubbed a little more fiercely.

"Ouch!" she squealed, hoping to be heard in the next room. "You're hurting me."

"No, I'm not. Keep still."

"Let me go!"

Her voice became shriller. He knew he could make her cry if he wanted to, any minute now. He could scrub a little harder, squeeze her arm a little tighter, pay her back. Instead, he released her and threw her a grubby towel to dry herself.

"Go and put that in the washing basket upstairs

and then come back and set the tray. I'll put the kettle on."

"Don't have to."

She watched him turn slowly towards her. He bent down so that his face was close to hers and spoke very quietly.

"No," he said. "You don't have to but, if you don't, when he's gone, I'll hit you so hard you won't know what day it is."

" 'S'not allowed," she said, but he needed to make her think that he might.

"Just try me," he said and saw a flicker of real doubt before she scampered away with the towel. A moment later she was back and Matt wondered where she had left it. He leaned against the sink and watched her standing on her toes to rummage in the drawer for teaspoons, and he had to resist the urge to take over as she arranged the crockery on the tray.

The tip of her tongue curled up under her top lip, a sign that she was concentrating very hard in an effort not to clash the cups against the saucers. She had already broken a china mug, a plate and a glass dish so far that week in her efforts to help

with the dishes. Matt suddenly wanted to gather
her up and say he was sorry but she would only
think she had won.

"Look, Titch. I've got to go to Mr Johal's at five.
You'll be a good girl till Mum gets back, won't
you? And no eating chocolates as soon as I've
gone." Sara ignored him. "D'you hear, Sara?
You're to behave yourself."

She didn't know what he was talking about. She was quite capable of being good for half an hour till Mum arrived. She did it every Friday.

"And you're not to go anywhere."

"We're going swimming."

"Later," Matt said firmly. "You're not to go out without Mum."

"But . . ."

"Promise!" Matt took her by the shoulders and made her look at him. "I mean it. Promise me."

"Cross my heart," she said and he knew that the promise would last only as long as it took for Ian to have one of his good ideas.

"I've got an idea," he would say. "Let's go sailing," or "Let's go shooting." He had taken them all on a boat ride down the river and Matt had wished he had stayed at home. Matt decided not to go the next time and Ian had taken 'the girls' to a fun-fair where he had won a goldfish at the rifle-range. Sara had carried it home in a plastic bag and later tipped it into a jam jar, the only container they had. That night Ian named it Mick after watching Michael Fish on the weather forecast. Two days later, when it died, Sara had cried. So much for good ideas!

★ ★ ★

"I'll carry the tray if you open the doors," he said and she shot out of the kitchen and back to Ian before he had time to say anything else. She was already sitting on his knee when Matt went in.

"Do you take sugar?" he enquired, very politely, as if Ian were a guest.

"No thanks," Ian said. "Just a dash of milk."

"I want lots of milk and two sugars," Sara said. She liked her tea pale, creamy and tepid. He knew exactly how to get it just right.

"How come you're here on Friday?" he asked, as casually as he could. Even so it sounded a bit rude. "I mean, Mum doesn't finish work until five."

Ian seemed to hesitate and then make up his mind.

"I suppose I might as well tell you now as later," he said. "It's been rather a special day. It looks like I've got a new job, as coach and assistant manager with my old Scottish club. They're Premier Division now." Ian could hardly stop smiling.

"Great!" Matt said yet his hand shook as he poured the tea.

"Course, I'll miss working at United," Ian admitted, "but you have to snap up a chance when it's offered, don't you?" Matt nodded. It was what Ian did best, what he had always done.

"I'm afraid I need to go and get changed," Matt said, suddenly smiling too. "I've got my paper round to do." On the way out he helped himself to a couple of chocolates.

Chapter 3

The nights were getting lighter. All through the winter he had been trudging to the shop in semi-darkness, worrying about leaving his sister, drawing the curtains before he left so that no passing stranger could glance in to see her sitting alone in front of the television. Tonight he thought he could smell spring in the air. There were even tiny green shoots pushing up in Mrs Anwar's window-box. The pavement flowed beneath his feet.

It wasn't far and he always liked the moment of entering the shop with its old-fashioned jangly bell and its spicy smells, but it was embarrassing to find Mrs Anwar in there. She and Mr Johal were

chattering away in rapid Urdu and Matt hated not being able to join in, but they switched to English as soon as they saw him.

"No Sara today," she said. He felt it was an accusation. She must have been worried. He should have gone round straightaway to explain and he hadn't. Now the excuses poured out.

"I'm sorry," he said. "Ian fetched her from school and we didn't know he was going to. She was meant to come to you. I should have told you earlier, when I got home. Sorry."

"Is OK," she said. "No problem." Matt liked the way she managed with just the important words.

She patted his arm. "Very nice man."

"Yeah," he said.

"How are you, Matthew? You are well?"

"Yes, thank you, Mr Johal."

"And your mother? She is well also?"

"Yes, thank you."

"And your sister? She is recovered from her fall?"

"Healing nicely, thank you."

"You take special care of her from now on, I think."

"Oh yes," he said. "I'll try."

Mr Johal slid the heavy canvas bag across the counter, signalling the end of the conversation, and Matt hoisted the strap across his shoulder and used his arms to support the weight from underneath. Almost every household on his patch ordered the local weekly paper. This was only the first batch, but at least he had a system. He had worked out that if he tackled his own street first he could, in the shortest possible distance, get rid of enough papers to make the bag manageable.

As he worked his way down one side and up the other, folding and posting, he felt useful and enjoyed the thought of the money he was earning. It wasn't a difficult job, though he was pleased that most of the residents in the street had retained the old front doors with waist-high letter-boxes. He had to bend down to deliver his mum's. It broke his rhythm. As he poked the paper through he heard Sara clattering up the stairs, probably using hands and feet in her usual monkey-like ascent. He was pleased to think of Ian being lumbered with her. She was excited and showing off. The street outside seemed quite peaceful in comparison and Matt decided to take his time.

He had two more roads to do before he went back for the second lot and the larger houses near the park took longer, having gardens and other hazards. Stiffly-hinged flaps threatened to snatch his fingers; overgrown bushes tried to snag his sweater. Number fifteen had an irritable little dog that snapped behind the front door or, worse still, if allowed out, would yap and leap at the gate, daring Matt to invade its territory. It hadn't bitten him yet but he'd thought of what he'd like to do if it did. Sure, it was the dog's own garden, but it still needed to be taught a lesson. He reckoned he could score quite a few points by lofting it over a couple of hedges. It reminded him of a rugby ball on legs and he imagined a graceful, curving flight into alien country.

And there was Mr Bradley at number twenty-one, who always tried to send him on errands to the neighbours. The old man never returned the things he borrowed and some people had been quite rude to Matt. He had learnt to post the paper and run.

* * *

By the time he turned back towards the shop again it was almost ten minutes to six. He wandered along practising a speech, wondering how to ask Mr Johal whether he could work any other evenings, perhaps helping in the shop or the store room. He would need more cash if he wanted to look after the family – especially if he hoped to come up with some good ideas of his own once Ian had moved on.

Mr Johal was standing outside the shop looking up and down the road. He beckoned urgently as soon as he caught sight of Matt who suddenly abandoned his plan and began to run. Mr Johal liked efficiency and reliability above all things and tonight, of all nights, Matt had let him down, dawdling around the streets as if he had all the time in the world.

"Sorry," he panted but Mr Johal propelled him towards the door.

"Come," he said. "It is your mother."

Inside his mother was waiting, her face flushed and anxious.

"Where the hell's Sara?" she said. "There's no answer at Mrs Anwar's. I thought she would be with you."

"No. She's at home," he said.

"Do you think I would be here if she were?" Matt saw it all in a flash – his mother coming home to an empty house, the bewilderment turning to panic as first she found the Anwars out and then the rush to the shop to see if he'd taken his sister with him.

"She's with Ian. They've gone swimming, I expect."

He watched the body sag with relief. "I did tell her not to until you got home. Isn't there a note?"

"I don't know. I didn't see one but I expect there is. I'll go and look." She turned to Mr Johal. "Sorry to bother you," and then back to Matt, lowering her voice. "What's Ian doing here? He didn't say he was coming over today." She obviously hadn't yet noticed the presents either and Matt wondered whether to tell her, but decided that it was the kind of news that Ian should deliver himself.

"I've only done half the papers," he said, changing the subject. "Do you want me to come home with you or . . ."

"No," she replied. "Finish your round. I'll see you later." She hurried out, giving Mr Johal a weak smile, embarrassed that he had been involved. She worried constantly about Sara being looked after properly. She'd have hated having to admit in public that she didn't know where her daughter was.

Matt lifted the second, even heavier bag that had been prepared for him and followed her out. He could murder Sara! Why could she never do as she was told? And Ian should have had more sense.

Chapter 4

By the time he had finished he was feeling tired and hungry. Mr Johal sometimes gave him something from the shop as well as his wages and Matt hoped it might be something he could eat on the way home. This time it was a packet of ginger biscuits.

"Thank you," he said. "I like these."

"For your mother," said Mr Johal, "and her friend. They will be at home now I think." So he had been taking it all in, thought Matt. "Not like Ayesha this time!" His employer smiled kindly.

"No," Matt replied. "Not this time."

Ayesha had been in his class at school when they had first moved here and she and her mother had been especially welcoming. Ayesha had given him a guided tour of the neighbourhood and for a few weeks they had been friends. In mentioning her just now, Mr Johal had meant to be reassuring, Matt knew, but as he hurried home, fingering the coins in his pocket, he wished he hadn't been reminded about all that.

The moment he tapped on the front door his mother was there to open it.

"I haven't found a note," she said. "I can't understand it."

"Aren't they back yet? It's nearly two hours." He pushed the door with his foot.

"Don't do that, stupid! You'll break the glass."

"No, I won't. It's special stuff. It's supposed to withstand wear and tear."

"Kicking it is not wear and tear," she said, "so don't do it again."

Matt picked up his schoolbag which had fallen on to the floor and threw it back on to the bottom step. "And you can take that up to your room right now before I break my neck over it."

"It's really good to be home," he muttered, but not too loudly. He knew she was snappy because

she was worried and she was worried because
neither Sara nor pea-brained Ian had thought about
how she would feel, not being sure where they had
gone. He took the bag and the biscuits upstairs.

When he came down again he tried to cheer her
up. "Sara's probably hungry after the pool," he
suggested. "I bet they're having something to eat."

"She hasn't taken her swimsuit. I've already
checked."

Matt felt a sudden pang of real concern. "Why
don't you ask around? Go and ask Mrs Zelazowski.
She's always watching through the curtains. She
might have seen them."

"Did Ian have the car?"

"I don't know. Didn't see it." Sometimes Ian had to park half-way down the road and sometimes even streets away. Spaces were hard to find. "Do you want *me* to go and ask Mrs Zelazowski?"

"No. I'll go," she said. "Someone will have seen them." But Mrs Zelazowski wasn't in and Mrs Anwar had seen nothing.

By the time she came back Matt was feeling uneasy. "Do you think we should ring the police?" he said.

"The police?"

"To find out if there's been an accident." He hadn't meant to scare her. "I mean in case they're in a traffic jam because of an accident."

"How long did you say they've been gone?" she asked.

"How long does it take?"

He wished he hadn't mentioned the police. He had only said it to see what she'd say. He had expected her to say "Don't be silly!" or "Of course not." He didn't know what else to suggest. When she spoke again she was thinking aloud. "It's not like Ian to disappear without saying something. I

just can't understand it."

"Stay here. I'll find someone who saw them. I won't be long and I bet they'll be back before me." She continued to peer into the darkening street. "Don't worry, Mum."

He should never have mentioned the word 'accident' but it was too late now. When they turned up safe and sound Ian would smile, apologize sweetly just like he did when he forgot her birthday, and she would even forgive this.

As he stepped out into the gloom again, Matt turned up the collar of his jacket and plunged his hands deep into his trouser pockets. He didn't know where to begin until he heard, in the distance, the shuddering hiss of a bus pulling up at the stop on the main road. He headed towards it, for no other reason than that there would be people coming home.

Chapter 5

It was just that time when the gathering dusk is draining the colour from the day and the springy feeling that he'd had earlier seemed to have diminished with the light. A white bundle in the road caught his eye, but it was only a discarded chip wrapper blown against a wheel. Kicking it aside, he noticed something shiny – a twenty pence piece like a tiny silver medal in the gutter. Pity it isn't a pound, he thought as he bent down to retrieve it, but then beggars can't be choosers, as his mother was fond of reminding him.

He noticed that Mr Anwar's old van needed new tyres. I bet Ian hasn't got bald tyres, he thought, and I bet he doesn't eat fish and chips from the paper. Ian ate in restaurants and paid his bills with a plastic card.

While he rubbed the coin on his sleeve Matt gazed all around, just in case Ian and Sara had turned into the street while he was bending down, but there was no sign. In fact there was no sign of anybody. Doors were closed. All the children had been called in.

Normally he quite liked walking the streets in the dark, when lamps glowed behind flimsy curtains, making cosy, coloured squares in the black walls. Sometimes people left their curtains open and you could see right in. He always glanced furtively, too embarrassed to peer but unable to resist a quick peek; yet now, just when he needed to find Sara, the whole neighbourhood seemed to have shut itself away.

The row of parked cars told him that beyond those brick walls there must be people, lots of private and separate little lives going on, but the houses presented identical blank faces, hiding their secrets. Matt wondered how the police began when people were reported missing. Supposing Ian had decided to leave for some reason and Sara had gone off on her own? Would she do that? He wasn't even sure where some of her friends lived.

It came to him that perhaps everyone knew something he didn't. What had he missed while he had been out on his paper round? A bomb scare? A gas leak? An escaped prisoner on the prowl? He had come out to make urgent enquiries and the population had melted away.

It was, therefore, a great relief when the aroma of chips drifted in on a sudden swoosh of wind. At least it meant there would be people and food. The hot, vinegary smell reminded him that he was starving and he quickened his stride, pacing the familiar pavements. If Sara had been at home he might well have been heading this way anyway. His mum would have offered them beans or egg on toast for supper and Sara would have followed her around, plucking at her sleeve, chanting "Chish and fips! Chish and fips!" until they couldn't stand it any more and were forced to give in.

Wes was in the chip shop with a cardboard box, ordering for the whole family.

"Hey Tommo!" he sang out. "How y' doin'?"

"OK," Matt replied. "Just fancied a few chips."

"Large chips for my mate," Wes told the new girl behind the counter. Matt didn't recognize her.

"Open with salt and vinegar," Matt said. "Thanks, Wes."

"Sure you can't come tomorrow?" Matt looked puzzled until he realized that Wes was still on about the match. After tonight it would be the last place on earth he'd want to go.

"I'm sure," Matt said. "You haven't seen my sister, have you? Tonight I mean."

"No. Don't think so." Wes didn't bother to ask for details. He was counting the greasy parcels into his box.

As Matt left the steamy warmth of the shop the evening seemed colder than he remembered but the chips were hot and comforting in his hand, almost too hot to eat. He stood for a moment, blowing on to them and using his teeth to guide them into his mouth so he wouldn't burn his lips. Glancing up across the roofs he noticed that the street lamps were on in the main road, some of them already golden and bright, one still pinky-red and struggling. It reminded him how late it was getting.

A man and a child, two dark ill-matched shapes, turned into the street and with their sudden appearance the tight knot inside him seemed to burst open. He hurried forward but quickly realized his mistake. The man, dragging the small girl by the hand, was far too small to be Ian. The girl, had she been Sara, would have been dancing along at his side. As if to confirm his suspicions, the man suddenly stopped and let himself and the child into a house, pushing her roughly in front of him. Father or kidnapper? Friend or foe? The knot re-tied itself.

He vowed there and then that he would not leave Sara alone ever again. Mr Johal would easily find someone else to deliver the papers. When Sara turned up he would promise never to abandon her, not even for twenty minutes, and with Ian gone at last it would be up to him to take care of her properly. He realized how ridiculous it was to be out in the dark, unsure of what to do next. Ian usually came and went by car. They could have gone anywhere.

He felt he should be with his mum but reasoned that if he raced home now they might still not be there. If, on the other hand, he walked round the block, with a brisk, purposeful but unhurried stride, that would give them time to materialize.

Queens Avenue ran parallel to Essex Street, where he lived, and although it sounded more attractive, the two roads were identical, each only wide enough for two cars. Parked vehicles reduced them to one lane so the locals had learnt to go up one and down the other. Ian knew the rules by now. He would be sure to drive down Queens Avenue first. Matt headed that way.

There were lights on in some of the downstairs rooms and Matt found himself peering in rudely, as well as checking every passing or parked car. In one house a woman was reaching up to close the curtains just as Matt turned to stare and she glowered crossly at him. Two rough-looking men came out of a door just ahead and Matt called to them. Normally he might have crossed the road.

"Excuse me. Have you seen a man and a little girl? She's six, with blonde hair."

"Sorry, son," said one. The other laughed unpleasantly. They weren't even interested.

Then a sudden squeal of brakes frightened him. A car, turning in to the street, shuddered to a stop and something black shot across the pavement in front of him and half-way up the wall to his left. There it disappeared totally. Matt craned forward only to find that the cat had entered a house through a broken window where the lower half of the pane had been carefully chipped away, leaving a jagged overhang above. Probably kids or squatters, Matt thought. It was clearly intended as a way in.

The house was empty and looked long-neglected

and a sour smell shocked him as he leaned towards
the black hole. He stepped back quickly. Grubby
paint was peeling from the door and he could only
just make out a number in faded figures – 13!
Thirteen Queens Avenue?

Ayesha's house!

He hadn't thought about her for years and now,
twice in an hour, she had surfaced, bobbing up into
his mind, into the world, like a warning. Once her
name had been spoken in every house, on every
street corner. The tale had ballooned and spread,
filling the shops, the classrooms and the
playgrounds until, eventually, overblown and
overtaken with new events, it had exhausted itself

and shrivelled away. First the newspapers, then the police and then even the people who had been her neighbours had let it rest. Her mother had moved and he, who had been one of her best friends, had almost forgotten her, had been surprised to hear Mr Johal mention her after all this time. The memories swept over him.

The first few days that Ayesha was absent from school nobody had taken much notice but then the teacher's questions had begun. "When did you last see her?" "What did you talk about?" "Did you see her talking to anyone?" Matt had met her mother in the street but she had walked straight past him, even when he'd said hello. No-one at school ever explained what had happened but Wes had heard his mother gossiping about it. "They say her dad took her. Gone abroad they reckon." Matt questioned his own mum. She didn't seem keen to explain either but in the end she tried.

"No-one really knows, Matty, but it looks like her father has taken her home with him. He lives far away, not just in another town like your dad but in another country. He came to see her after school and now they're both gone." Matt had struggled to

understand. Ayesha hadn't said anything to him about leaving.

Even then Ayesha's story had disturbed him. Apart from missing her for a little while, he'd also become nervous of that unexpected knock at the door or the tall figure at the school gate. His own mum and dad lived in different places too, and he had waited, scared and excited, for his father to come for him, as he surely would. On the days when he had been miserable at school or cross with his mum and the baby, Matt had been sure that he would go; his dad would only have to ask. That would show them! Other days he would find himself planning a speech, trying to explain why he had to stay with Mum and Sara, why he was truly grateful but unable to leave. His father would be broken-hearted but would understand and they'd be together again one day.

In the end, as the months and years had passed, he had never had to make that terrible choice. Looking for his father in the crowd of parents outside school had given way to not looking (just in case the hoping had been preventing it) and then to not even thinking about it much, until tonight. The divorce had been so long ago that he could hardly remember what his father looked like and tonight, in the end, it was Sara, not himself, who had been unexpectedly collected from school. Of course, his father would never have come for Sara. He had hardly known her, just as Ian would never have thought of coming for him.

Suddenly Matt knew! He screwed the chip paper into a tight ball, hurled it through the broken window and began to pelt along the street. It had been nearly two and a half hours. There was a phone-box near the park gates but he decided to make one last check before calling the police; his mother would have to be told. His feet, in trainers, made rapid little thuds on the concrete while his head pounded with a vision of Sara, proud as a duchess, in the front seat of Ian's sleek convertible, being whisked away to who knows what, while Ian fed her chocolates and told her lies.

Chapter 6

He knew as soon as he walked in that nothing had changed.

"Any luck?" she said. He shook his head.

"Any news?"

"No. I can't understand it. I just can't understand it."

"Let me ring the police, Mum. You know you're worried sick." She shook her head and he couldn't bear it any more. "For heaven's sake! He's gone off with my sister and you're just letting him do it. They're probably long gone by now."

"Matthew! Whatever do you mean?" She was horrified. He hadn't meant to say it, not straight out like that, but it couldn't be unsaid. He found himself trying to explain and making it worse.

"Well, we might as well face it. It's always been Sara, right from the start, hasn't it? He probably couldn't face leaving her behind."

"Leaving her behind? What on earth are you talking about?"

"He's leaving this dump. Going to Scotland, or so he said. He told me."

"That's not until next season, and why would he want to take Sara and not us?"

"You still don't see, do you?"

"No, I don't." She was shouting at him now. "You can't seriously be suggesting what I think you're suggesting."

It was hopeless. He'd never persuade her. He'd have to make the phone call himself. It was probably too late already.

He turned towards the door and immediately a great shadow fell across it. He had it open in a moment and there she stood, a tiny subdued figure, half-supported by Ian's hand. Ian had his back to the doorway and seemed to be signalling to a departing taxi that was already sliding away down the street, but he whirled round and picked her up

in one continuous movement. As he lifted her Matt
saw that she had a bandage around her head, under
her fringe, and that one eye looked swollen and
bruised. He stepped aside and Ian seemed to
explode into the house.

"Oh, my love, I'm so sorry," he said, handing
her to her mother. "I phoned every Anwar in the
book but it was never the right one. I wish you'd let
me get a phone put in. I was going out of my mind
at the hospital. I couldn't leave her. She was so
scared, all that blood and then those strange people
prodding her around. I knew you'd be going crazy
but they kept saying they wouldn't be long, but
they were, and then the taxi took ages to come."

Sara hugged her mother as she was carried into the living room. Matt shut the door quietly and took off his coat. He thought about escaping upstairs but he wanted to know what had happened so he stood silently in the hall, holding his breath, and strained to listen. He could picture it, the two of them, heads close together, bending over Sara who would be nestling at the heart of it all, in her mother's arms.

"She's worn out," Ian said softly, "but she'll be fine. It's only a small cut but you know how head wounds bleed. I was scared she might have concussion."

"What happened?"

"She fell down the stairs. Got her foot caught in Matt's bag I think and went head over heels. I thought she'd cracked her head open. I just grabbed a towel off the stairs but I couldn't stop the blood. I dashed out and Mr Thing from next door . . ."

"Zelazowski?"

"Yes, him. He took us to the hospital. He was just off on his night shift." There was a moment's silence and then Ian's voice again. "It was all so fast but I should have left you a message somehow."

"It's all right now," she said. "Let me put her to bed and then we'll talk. Come on, Titch. Up the wooden hills!"

For once Sara didn't protest and Matt sidled into the kitchen as he heard them move towards the door.

"I've got the kettle on," Matt said as Ian appeared in the doorway. "For Sara's hot-water bottle. Would you like some tea or coffee?"

"You bet. I've gone all weak at the knees. Was your mum frantic?"

"She was getting a bit worried," Matt said, choosing the right words carefully. "It's lucky you came back when you did."

"I half-expected you to turn up at the hospital when it got so late," Ian went on. "I thought there might have been blood stains in the hall."

"Blood stains? We didn't see any stains."

"What's this?" said his mother, appearing with the hot-water bottle. "It's a good job we didn't notice, isn't it, Matt? We might have thought you had murdered her." Matt busied himself with the coffee jar and pretended he hadn't heard. Ian chuckled.

"Well, I admit that I'm tempted sometimes, but I dare say she'll improve. Girls do! How is she now?"

"Snuggled around Teddy and nearly asleep."

Matt took the rubber bottle and poured in the hot water, topping it up from the cold tap. In the dark window he saw their reflections as Ian folded his mother into his arms.

"Are you OK?" she asked tenderly.

"No. I'm starving," Ian replied. "Aren't you?"

"I'll cook you something," she said.

"What about a take-away?"

"What do you fancy?"

"How about fish and chips?" Ian suggested.

"I'll go," said Matt. "What shall I get?"

"No. I'll go," Ian insisted. "I don't want you out on the streets at this time of night. There are lots of strange people about. I won't be long."

"Well?" said his mum the moment she heard the door click.

"Well what?"

"Don't you think you owe him an apology?"

"He doesn't know what I said."

"Then you owe me an apology."

"Sorry."

Matt thought he had got away with it but she was only pausing for breath.

"You've never liked him, have you? What's he done to make you think such awful things?"

"I was just worried about Sara." It didn't seem enough. "And I was thinking about Ayesha."

"Oh, I see." That seemed to satisfy her for a minute but then she began again. "Well, my lad, perhaps you could try to be a little more welcoming in future. Please try, Matty. He's so kind. You must know that he wouldn't hurt any of us, ever."

"Shall I take Sara's bottle up?" he said.

* * *

Sara was already asleep but he tucked the bottle under the bedclothes anyway so that she could find it with her feet. Even in the dim glow of the nightlight he could see the bruised swelling below the bandage. She looked so little and frail. He could hardly bear to look at her, damaged yet again. She drove him mad most of the time but she needed protecting. Tonight she had needed urgent help and he hadn't been there. It was a good job that someone had!

He had been so pleased at the prospect of Ian's departure. Now he felt it might be like a safety-net being withdrawn. He had been so scared when he had thought that Sara had been taken. Now he couldn't believe he had actually thought it. Most of all he wished he had kept his thoughts to himself and, when he heard Ian return, he suddenly felt that he couldn't go down and face him. Eventually they had to call him.

"Matt? This food is going cold. Are you coming?" His knees cracked as he stood up. He had been kneeling on the lino by Sara's bed and they hurt as he straightened.

"Do you think that she will ever calm down?" he heard Ian say as he crept quietly downstairs. "Will she ever be sensible like Matt?"

"Who knows?" his mum replied. "Can you get that lucky twice?"

Matt took a deep shuddering breath. What was it she had said? "Try to be a bit more welcoming?" He launched himself into the room. "Aw, great!" he said. "Chish and fips!"